The First Air Voyage in the United States

The Story of Jean-Pierre Blanchard

written and illustrated by

ALEXANDRA WALLNER

Holiday House/New York

Library of Congress Cataloging-in-Publication Data
Wallner, Alexandra.
The first air voyage in the United States : the story of Jean-
Pierre Blanchard / by Alexandra Wallner. — 1st ed.
p.   cm.
Summary: Recounts the voyage of an eighteenth-century French
aeronaut by hot air balloon from Philadelphia to Woodbury, New
Jersey, in 1793.
ISBN 0-8234-1224-5 (hardcover : alk. paper)
1. Blanchard, Jean-Pierre, 1753–1809—Juvenile literature.
2. Balloon ascensions—Pennsylvania—Philadelphia—History—18th
century—Juvenile literature. [1. Blanchard, Jean-Pierre,
1753–1809. 2. Balloon ascensions.] I. Title.
TL620.B6W35   1996   95-20880   CIP   AC
629.13'0973—dc20

For the people
who help me fly ~
&
especially for

Margery Cuyler
and the Folks at
Holiday House

My name is Jean-Pierre Blanchard. I was born in Adelys, France, on July 4, 1753. When I was a boy, I dreamed of flying in the air, free like the birds.

I tried to fly like them, too. Even though I was not successful, I never stopped trying.

In 1781, I built my *vaisseau volant*, a flying machine. It was a giant balloon with four big wings at the bottom. I operated them with hand and foot levers.

Vaisseau Volant de M. BLANCHARD

Imagine my disappointment when I tried to demonstrate my new machine for my friends and it didn't work!

I knew, however, that someday I would succeed.

In 1783, the Montgolfier brothers, Jacques-Etienne and Joseph-Michel, built a hot-air balloon. They put a sheep, a rooster, and a duck in the basket and sent it up. The balloon rose fifteen hundred feet in the air and traveled two miles in eight minutes.

I was lucky that the flight was a success. King Louis XVI, Queen Marie Antoinette, and the whole royal court were watching.

Some months later, two men named Jean-François Pilâtre de Rozier and the Marquis François d'Arlandes took a ride in the brothers' balloon. They were the first people to fly in a balloon.

Jean-François Pilâtre de Rozier

Marquis François d'Arlandes

Alas, I wish *I* had been the first.

I was so enthusiastic about flying, I wanted to share it with people everywhere. I built my own balloon and made my first flight in Germany at Frankfurt am Main.

Going up was fun. Once I was in the air, however, it was an adventure finding a safe place to land. Sometimes, I was not lucky.

But my most famous European flight was crossing the English Channel. The flight was called the Eighth Wonder of the World.

England

Start of voyage

English Channel

End of voyage

France

Dr. John Jeffries of Boston flew with me.

All together, I made forty-four flights in Europe. But more than anything, I wanted to fly in America. Ever since the American Revolution, I admired the Americans' free spirit. I wanted a chance to fly where the people were as free as the birds.

On January 9, 1793, I got my chance. I had arranged to fly from Philadelphia, the capital of the United States at the time, to Woodbury, New Jersey. Many people from Philadelphia and beyond came to watch. Some of them were important politicians and their wives.

President George Washington gave me a letter that explained to the people of Woodbury who I was. Since I spoke no English, I was glad to have the letter.

Rebel, a friend's dog, was to travel with me.

Cannons fired, bands played, and crowds cheered as my balloon took off and rose higher and higher. Rebel was quite nervous.

The Delaware River looked like a ribbon. Clouds were like wispy cobwebs. I could have just enjoyed the ride, but I had agreed to perform experiments for some scientist friends.

Dr. Wistar had filled six small bottles with liquids. He asked me to pour out the liquids and recork the bottles with air from the highest point of my flight. He wanted to examine what the air was like far away from earth.

Dr. Glentworth asked me to weigh a stone. On the ground, it had weighed 5½ ounces. It weighed 4 ounces in the air.

Dr. Rush asked me to take my pulse at the highest point, which was 5,812 feet. My pulse up there was ninety-two per minute. On the ground, it was eighty-four.

After my experiments were completed, I enjoyed eating a cookie.
Rebel was happy to have a cookie, too.

We drifted into a flock of pigeons.

Rebel barked and jumped high.

A gust of wind tilted the balloon.

We were now over the woods of New Jersey. I prepared to land. I locked my equipment, which consisted of a thermometer, barometer, scale, second watch, and the small bottles, all kept in a box. I did not want anything to break.

I looked for an open space in the woods. By now, I had become experienced at landing, and we touched ground with only a little bump. I had completed the voyage in exactly forty-six minutes.

I had made the first successful air voyage in the United States. Rebel
was happy to be on the ground again.

A frightened farmer saw me land and ran into the woods. I could not understand what he was shouting. I wanted to show him the letter from President Washington.

Other farmers came toward me. One of them read the letter. The farmers were quite impressed because they loved their president.

The farmers deflated the balloon and carried it to an inn.

There they put the balloon into a wagon. I was given a spirited horse to take me back to Philadelphia. Since the country road was rough, I wish I could have returned to the city in my balloon.

When I arrived in Philadelphia, I went to President Washington. I thanked him for his letter of introduction. It had traveled by air from Philadelphia to New Jersey, thereby becoming the first air-mail letter in America. I was the first person to fly in America.

And Rebel was the first dog.

Author's Note

Jean-Pierre's air voyage from Philadelphia to Woodbury was his forty-fifth flight. I made up the name Rebel for the dog.

Jean-Pierre returned to Europe, where he made fifteen more flights. His wife was also an aeronaut.

During his sixtieth flight—in 1808, over The Hague in the Netherlands—he became ill. He died in 1809.

Jean-Pierre is known as the Greatest of the Early Aeronauts.

Most of the information for this book came from *The First Air Voyage in America*, published by the Penn Mutual Life Insurance Co., Independence Square, Philadelphia, 1943.

Pronunciation Guide

(The following guide is not exact, since the French language has different sounds from those of English.)

Bonjour aux oiseaux!: Bawn-jour ohs wah-so! (Good morning to the birds!)

Jean-Pierre Blanchard: Shawn Pee-air Blawn-shard

Adelys: Ah-deh-leese

En haut!: Un oh! (Up!)

Un, deux, trois . . . Sautez-vous.: On, dih, twa . . . Sot-tay voo. (One, two, three . . . Jump.)

Il croit qu'il puisse voler!: Il cwa keel pweese voh-lay! (He thinks he can fly!)

Attention, Jean-Pierre!: Ah-tahn-shun, Shawn Pee-air!: (Be careful, Jean-Pierre!)

J'ai une idée, Maman.: Shay oon ee-day, Mah-maw. (I have an idea, Mother.)

Vaisseau volant: Veh-so vo-lahn (flying ship)

Sacré bleu!: sack-cray bleu! (Holy blue!)

Ça va: Sah-vah. (All is well.)

Pauvre Jean-Pierre. Il fait de son mieux.: Pauv-reh Shawn Pee-air. Il fay dih son mee-yih. (Poor Jean-Pierre. He tries his best.)

Je reviens!: Jeu reh-vyen! (I'll be back!)

Ja!: Ya! (German for "yes.")

Sie sehen gut aus, Herr Blanchard!: Zee zay-hen goot owse, Hair Blawn-shard! (German for "Looking good, Mr. Blanchard!")

Merci Bien, Monsieur le Président: Mare-see bee-yan, Meu-see-yer lih Pray-zee-daunt. (Thank you, Mr. President.)

Hourra! Nous l'avons fait!: Oo-rah! Noo lav-on fay! (Hooray! We did it!)

Qu'est-ce qu'il y a?: Kess keel-ee-ah? (What's up?)

Je m'appelle Monsieur Blanchard.: Jeu mah-pel Meu-see-yer Blawn-shard. (My name is Mr. Blanchard.)